THE PUZZLE CLUB™
MUSICAL
MYSTERY

by Dandi Daley Mackall

Based on characters developed for *The Puzzle Club Christmas Mystery*, an original story by Mark Young for Lutheran Hour Ministries

Lutheran Hour
Ministries

CPH
SAINT LOUIS

Puzzle Club™ Mysteries
The Puzzle Club Christmas Mystery
The Puzzle Club Mystery of Great Price
The Puzzle Club Case of the Kidnapped Kid
The Puzzle Club Poison-Pen Mystery
The Puzzle Club Musical Mystery

Cover illustration by Mike Young Productions

Scripture quotations are from the King James or Authorized Version of the Bible.

Copyright © 1998 International Lutheran Laymen's League

™ Trademark of International Lutheran Laymen's League

Published by Concordia Publishing House
3558 S. Jefferson Avenue, St. Louis, MO 63118-3968
Manufactured in the United States of America

2 3 4 5 6 7 8 9 10   07 06 05 04 03 02 01 00 99 98

Contents

music with words written between the staffs. "Everybody will try out using the same song," he explained. "Hang on to this. My music keeps disappearing. If I didn't know better, I'd think someone's hiding my songs."

Alex stared at the words and the notes. Sing? Him? How had he let Korina push him into this?

"It will be such fun, Alex," Korina said. "*This* song is one the boy lead sings while he's waiting for his girlfriend. He hears noises and gets scared, so he sings the song to take his mind off his fear. Christopher has written a show of professional quality, Alex. You should be proud to take part."

Alex was feeling a lot of things, but proud wasn't one of them.

"Mostly the play is just songs," Christopher explained. "But Tobias says the money we raise from selling tickets will go a long way toward keeping the Youth Center open. Hey, there's Ms. Dusic," Christopher said, pointing to the band shell. "I better see if she's ready to start."

Alex couldn't think straight. What was he doing? He couldn't sing—couldn't carry a tune in a bucket, his grandmother always said.

"Don't worry, Alex," Korina said, as if reading his thoughts. "I'm no singer either. But The Puzzle Club has to stick together."

"Hey, who's that old woman?" asked a boy, pushing his way between Alex and Korina. It was Will Sanders, a boy in Korina's class.

"It is not polite to point, Will," Korina said. "That is Ms. Dusic. It rhymes with *music*. She's in charge of music for Christopher and Tobias' play. She's handling the auditions."

"Why?" asked Will. "She's so old."

"Ms. Dusic grew up here," Korina explained. "I think she went to school with Tobias. My mother told me Ms. Dusic left to direct a symphony in New York. She lived there until her husband died."

Alex knew about Ms. Dusic. She could sing and play the piano and every instrument ever invented. Patrick Grimaldi, the sheriff's son, called her Madam Music Dusic.

Will shrugged. "Well, I'm trying out for the lead. I hope her hearing's good. If she can hear me, she'll pick me."

Alex hoped Will was as good as he thought he was. Will played the trumpet, so maybe he could sing too. Alex didn't really think he was in danger of getting a part. He'd just have to get tough enough to make it through the tryout. Then that would be that. Alex looked Will over—he wore a torn, dirty shirt and faded blue jeans. *At least Will could have washed his face,* Alex thought. Maybe Ms. Dusic wouldn't notice.

"Ladies and gentlemen! Could I please have—" The microphone squealed and wiped out Ms. Dusic's greeting. It sounded like someone scratching a blackboard. People in the crowd covered their ears until the microphone stopped screeching.

"Can you hear me now?" Ms. Dusic called.

Alex stared up at the heavyset, cello-shaped, gray-haired woman. She wore a black hat with a fake daisy sticking out the top.

"Welcome to the auditions for our first annual musical, *Musical Monster Madness.*" Ms. Dusic's voice sounded almost like she was singing opera. "Ah, there's Tobias." She waved a yellow scarf at him. "Tobias, would you please say a few words?"

Tobias turned bright red as he climbed the steps of the band shell. "Th-thank you," he said. He let out a sigh that traveled over the microphone like a breeze through the town square. "We plan to use the ticket money to keep the Youth Center open. God has used that center to help a lot of kids discover how much Jesus loves them. You see—"

Ms. Dusic shoved in front of Tobias and started clapping. "Thank you, Tobias," she said.

Tobias smiled, then hurried off the stage. Alex watched, admiring his white-haired friend. Tobias never missed a chance to talk about Jesus—even though he looked as scared as Alex felt.

"Now," said Ms. Dusic, "we will begin with auditions for the female roles." She called a name from her list, "Tonya?"

Tonya sang so softly, Alex could hardly hear her. He thought he might try that. If he sang softly, it wouldn't be like singing at all. He'd just mouth the words.

Girl after girl sang the same song. Alex thought they all sounded pretty much the same. When it was Korina's turn, she held the music in front of her face. Alex decided she hadn't been kidding. She really wasn't a singer. But at least she'd had the guts to get up there. And he knew she'd never let him live it down if he did not try.

Ms. Dusic announced the male tryouts. Josh sang. Then Danny. Alex had to get out of there. His legs felt wobbly, like limp noodles. He was not just chicken. He was worse than chicken! Chicken and noodles? Alex was chicken soup. He just couldn't go through with this. And he didn't care if Korina teased him about it for the rest of his life.

"Alex?" Tobias put his hand on Alex's shoulder. "I want to tell you how proud I am that you're helping with Christopher's play. It's a wonderful thing you Puzzle Club detectives are doing for all the children at the center."

"About the musical, Tobias," Alex said, "I don't …"

"Shh-h-h," Tobias said. Then he whispered, "Look who's trying out now. It's Will. Now there's a boy I pray will come to the center. Maybe you'll get a chance to talk to him about it while you both work on the play."

Will sang so loudly, he really didn't need the microphone. "I wonder what that noise is," he sang. "The thing that I fear most/is somewhere lurks a monster or a phantom or a ghost." Each word came across clear and crisp, and he had a good voice.

Alex started to relax. Will wouldn't have any trouble winning the lead role.

Suddenly the microphone cut out. Christopher ran to the mike. Then the lights in the park dimmed and fizzled out. "Nobody move!" Christopher shouted.

Alex could make out the forms of Christopher and Korina as they disappeared behind the band shell. A couple of minutes passed during which the crowd murmurs grew louder. At last the lights clicked on. The mike squealed. And Will started singing right where he had left off.

Christopher and Korina joined Tobias and Alex.

"What happened?" Tobias asked.

Christopher looked puzzled. "I'm not sure, Tobias. Somebody disconnected the wires to the sound and light systems."

Korina held out a black cord with cut wires. "And if you ask me," she said, "this was no accident."

2

From Bad to Worse

Alex was just going to suggest canceling auditions when he heard his name over the loudspeaker.

All eyes turned toward him. Tobias and Korina pushed Alex up the stairs. Then he was standing in front of the microphone, the crowd staring up at him.

Alex tried to swallow. He heard a baby crying somewhere in the back of the crowd. Murmuring voices mixed like TV noise from another room. A little kid in the front row chewed gum, then popped a giant bubble.

"Go ahead, Alex," Ms. Dusic sang in a loud whisper.

Alex heard the music begin. It was the same song he'd just heard Will and the others sing. He glanced down and was surprised to see the sheet music in his hands. He cleared his throat. The piano started over. It was so loud that the stage shook.

Alex opened his mouth. Something came out. He mouthed the words. Then he heard himself as an echo through the loudspeakers.

Alex peeked behind him at Ms. Dusic. He glanced to stage left. Christopher winked. He looked stage right. Korina mouthed the lines from behind the curtain. If anything, his terror grew. Until … finally, the music stopped.

Alex dropped the music and took off. He raced down the stairs of the band shell and through the roaring laughter of the audience. He heard his name called, but he didn't slow down or turn around.

Alex didn't stop running until he'd crossed the street and reached Puzzleworks. Tobias had left the door to his store unlocked, and Alex slipped inside. Moonlight streamed through the Puzzleworks' windows and fell on puzzles of every size and shape.

Alex looked around, glad that nobody was there. He'd never be able to show his face again. He had to be the worst singer in the whole world. And everybody had laughed at him. This was one Puzzle Club project that would have to go on without any help from him. He could imagine what Ms. Dusic would say about him.

A flapping noise made Alex spin around, his fists raised. Sherlock, The Puzzle Club's parakeet, landed on Alex's shoulder.

"Hey, Sherlock," Alex said. "You're the only friend I have left. And that's just because Tobias wouldn't let you come to tryouts." He stroked the bird's soft green head. "Let's hide out at headquarters."

"*Braawk! Hide out!*" screeched Sherlock.

Alex pulled the thick, gold cord behind Tobias' counter. In answer, one of the shelves of puzzles slid to the side. An arched doorway appeared with steps leading up. Alex climbed the secret stairway, punched in the security code, and entered Puzzle Club headquarters.

Usually Christopher had his camera stuff spread all over and Korina's experiments hogged half of the room. But today paper lay scattered over every table and chair. The wastebaskets overflowed with wadded paper. Christopher had turned one corner of the attic into a stage.

Alex didn't like it one bit. "Christopher's *Musical Monster Madness* is ruining head-quarters!" he told Sherlock. "Did Korina and Christopher forget we're The Puzzle Club *detectives*? What's a detective doing working on a musical anyway?"

Alex crossed the room to his favorite spot—the long, metal clothes rack. To his relief, everything looked exactly like he'd left it. Alex's costumes hung from the metal bar. Hats, scarves, wigs, and other disguises were piled on top of the rack or crammed into his trunk.

"I need a great disguise, Sherlock," Alex said, pushing hangers aside and examining clothes. "Something so perfect nobody will recognize me."

He considered the army uniform, the navy double-breasted suit, the ringmaster's tuxe-do, a cowboy outfit. "No, no, no," Alex said after each one. This disaster called for an all-new creation.

Alex opened the trunk at his feet. He took out petroleum jelly, actor's face glue, a mus-tache, and a wax bump. Using the mirror on the inside of the trunk's lid, Alex went to work.

16

First, he smoothed his hair down as much as possible, running his fingers through it until some of the waves turned straight. Next, he scooped some actor's glue onto his upper lip and pressed the mustache in place. The wax bump he stuck under his bottom lip. For a hat, Alex chose a French beret.

Alex studied his new look in the mirror. "Ah, Sherlock," he said, "eet eez chust parfait!" He'd have to work on his French accent, but he thought he could pull it off.

"Oui, oui!" came a voice from behind him.

Alex jumped. The trunk lid slammed shut. Sherlock flew off, squawking. "*Oui, oui! Braawk!*"

Alex turned around and saw Korina grinning from ear to ear. "Korina!" he said, ashamed he hadn't heard her sneak up on him. "What do *you* want?"

"To congratulate you, Alex," Korina said. She actually held out her hand to shake his.

"Very funny, Korina," Alex said, ignoring her outstretched hand. He opened the trunk again and felt inside for the right jacket.

"No, really, Alex," Korina said. "First, Ms. Dusic announced the girls who got parts in

Christopher's play: Tonya, Cora, April, Katy, and …"

Up the stairs came more footsteps. *Great,* Alex thought. *Let's get everybody in here to make fun of me. I should sell popcorn!*

Christopher joined Korina. "And Korina!" he said, patting her on the back. "Ms. Dusic picked Korina to play the part of the day ghost. She gets to sing 'Something's Spooky' with Will."

"That's nice. Congratulations, Korina." Alex knew he didn't sound any more excited than he felt. But what did they expect? Cartwheels? Why couldn't they just leave him alone?

"Will wasn't very happy about it," Korina said. "He was hoping he'd get to sing a solo."

Now Alex turned to face them. "Didn't he get the lead? I thought Will did the best job singing."

"Well," Christopher said, not looking Alex in the eyes. "So did I, to tell the truth."

Korina chimed in. "And so did Will! You should have seen him when Ms. Dusic announced the results. Will kicked over two chairs. Tobias had to calm him down."

18

"But Ms. Dusic had a different idea about who should star in *Musical Monster Madness*," Christopher continued. "She thought Will was good and all—and he still gets a part in the play—but she thought somebody else was perfect for the lead."

Alex shrugged and went back to searching through his trunk. He didn't really care who got the lead. He knew *he* wouldn't be going to the play—not even for Tobias or the Youth Center.

"Indeed," Korina said. "Ms. Dusic said that the individual who got the part played it perfectly. He acted scared, just like the part demanded. He made his voice shake and was so convincing, she had to give the part ... to *you!*"

"That's nice," Alex said. "I'm sure he'll ..." Alex stopped. Slowly he turned toward Christopher and Korina. "Who?"

"You, Alex!" Christopher said. "Isn't that great? Ms. Dusic went on and on about you. She thinks you're a real actor!"

"*Braawk! You!*" Sherlock repeated, swooping back and forth across Puzzle Club headquarters. "*Oui, oui! Braawk!*"

This couldn't be happening. There'd been a horrible mistake!

Tobias appeared in the doorway, out of breath. "I had to congratulate you, Alex," he said. "I'm so proud of the way you detectives are supporting the Youth Center." The bell rang downstairs, and Tobias left to answer it.

"Won't it be great?" Korina said. "The whole Puzzle Club working on *Musical Monster Madness.*"

"Wait," Alex started. "I can't ..."

But Korina and Christopher were already heading for the secret passage. Christopher stuck two rolls of film into his pocket. Korina pushed the wall button with The Puzzle Club logo on it—a magnifying glass and a giant eyeball. Instantly the glass eyeball opened to reveal a tunnel slide.

Korina climbed onto the slide. "Rehearsals begin tomorrow morning, Alex. Eight o'clock. Don't be late!" She pushed off and slid down the chute, banging the metal sides as she went.

This was the worst thing that had ever happened to Alex. He'd already made a complete fool of himself. And now this! Things couldn't possibly get any worse.

Then they did. "8 A.M.!" Christopher called over his shoulder as he climbed onto the secret slide. "At The Gleason."

"The *what?*" Alex yelled after him.

But Christopher was already clanging down the slide, halfway to the alley by now.

The Gleason? Talk about worse! Alex shivered as he pictured the crumbled, dark, run-down, ex-opera house in the West End. *The Gleason!* Everybody who was anybody knew for a fact—The Gleason was haunted!

3

The Weather Outside Is Frightful!

At 7:30 the next morning, Alex pedaled toward the West End. Sherlock dug his claws into Alex's shoulder as they bumped over railroad tracks in semidarkness. "How did I get myself into this mess, Sherlock?" Alex asked. Then he remembered. "Puck, puck, puck," he muttered, picturing Korina's chicken imitation.

"*Puck, puck ... braawk ... puck!*" squawked Sherlock, flapping his wings in Alex's face.

"Aw, pipe down," Alex said. And now what was he doing? Biking through the worst neighborhood in the city to the scariest place he could imagine. Alex didn't know which terrified him more—singing on stage or rehearsing in the old, haunted Gleason.

Except for a truck now and then, the streets seemed deserted. Alex biked past boarded-up warehouses. Store after store stood empty, their front windows broken, as if the owners had escaped by jumping through the glass panes.

A clap of thunder exploded so loud that Alex felt his bike shake.

"*Squawk!*" Sherlock burrowed down the neck of Alex's jacket until only his beak poked out from the collar.

Alex thought about turning back, but one look at the dark clouds changed his mind. He'd never make it home before the storm hit. He could see the Youth Center in the next block. That meant The Gleason would be in the block after that. He'd just as soon get off these deserted streets as fast as possible.

A long, mud-spitting truck zoomed around the corner. Alex swerved up onto the sidewalk to get out of the truck's path, nearly hitting a broad, wooden sign. The truck, loaded with heads of lettuce, kept going, leaving Alex panting. "Crazy driver!" he yelled after the truck.

Alex leaned against the sign to catch his breath. Behind him was a crumbled brick building. Alex looked down and read the painted, black letters on the sign: "New Greater City Shopping Mall Coming Soon! Riley Developers."

"Yeah, right," Alex said. Who would ever come down here to buy anything? Except for The Gleason and the Youth Center, there were no businesses open.

Jagged lightning streaked the purplish sky, and the clouds opened. Rain fell in wavy sheets. In a few seconds Alex was soaked through to the bone.

Keeping his head down, Alex pedaled hard. When he looked up, the domed roof of the spooky Gleason loomed before him. An empty, tattered marquee dangled over the front entrance.

Alex wheeled his bike to the side of the building. All along the brick wall, gangs had spray-painted ownership. If he left his bike outside, it might get stolen. Pushing through a side door, Alex pulled his bike inside after him. As far as Alex knew, ghosts didn't ride bikes.

Inside, The Gleason looked like a giant movie theater with seats spread in three main sections. To Alex's right was the stage, a dark, heavy curtain drawn all the way across. To his left, a balcony hung over the back of the auditorium.

Leaning his bike against the nearest wall, Alex called out, "Hello! Is anybody here? Tobias?"

"*Braawk!*" came the answer from inside his coat.

"Sherlock!" Alex said, unzipping his wet jacket. "I forgot about you."

The parakeet flew out of Alex's jacket, circled above his head, then zoomed straight for the stage.

Alex didn't want to budge from the door. He might have to make a quick getaway. "Sherlock!" he yelled.

Alex's voice bounced back at him from the barren walls of the old Gleason. *Sherlock! Sherlock! Sherlock!* It was almost like ghosts were making fun of him, mocking his cries.

"Hey! Somebody!" Alex yelled. Where was everybody anyway? Tobias was always on time. No matter how mad Alex was at Sherlock for flying off, he couldn't leave the bird to the mercy of whatever lurked in this theater. "Come back, you loony bird!" he cried. The floorboards squeaked as Alex started toward the stage. A musty mildew hung in the air so thick that Alex could feel it.

Sherlock swooped from the stage down a side aisle. Then he soared across the seats toward the back of the theater. Alex chased after the squawking parakeet. He stumbled in the aisle. A thin beam of light seeped through a loose board in the balcony. Alex reached the back of the theater but lost Sherlock. "Where are you, you flying feathered …"

Alex stopped. He listened. Only the faint noise of a city waking up came through the walls of The Gleason. Tires splashed through puddles. Horns honked as a stoplight clicked green. But inside The Gleason, an eerie silence sent a chill down his spine. And Sherlock was nowhere in sight.

Suddenly, something swooped out from behind a door. Thunder rumbled and clapped at that same instant. Alex screamed. Then Sherlock flew to his shoulder.

This was ridiculous. What was he doing here? "Hey!" Alex hollered, his voice echoing around the theater. "Where is everybody?"

He knew he'd pedaled fast—but not that fast. Everybody couldn't be late. It had to be way past eight o'clock.

Alex's mind began to race. Rain pounded the roof. Thunder shook the windowpanes. What if everybody had already been there, but something had happened to them? Something awful. What if the ghosts of The Gleason didn't like Christopher's *Musical Monster Madness?* What if they'd taken their revenge?

"Tobias? Christopher? Korina? Ms. Dusic?" Alex cried.

Nothing.

Thunder crashed. Then, just as it died down, Alex thought—no, he was sure—he heard something strange. "Oooooh!" A high-pitched, eerie moan rose from somewhere onstage. Except nobody was there.

"I-I-Is s-somebody there?" Alex asked weakly.

In answer, the moan grew louder. This time it sounded like, "Boooooo!"

Alex was shaking, and not from the cold and rain. He still didn't see anyone onstage. The faded, blood-red velvet curtain was still drawn across it. Alex called louder, "Who's there? You're not scaring me. My friends will be here any minute."

Alex slinked behind one of the theater seats in the second-to-last row. Maybe whatever it was wouldn't see him.

But Sherlock had other ideas. "*Booo! Braawk!*" he squawked.

Alex tried to grab the parakeet. "No, Sherlock! Come back!" he screamed.

The bird darted through the opening between the curtains. Alex raced down the aisle after him. The eerie voice groaned again. And this time The Gleason ghost's cry stopped Alex in his tracks.

"Boooo!" came the voice. "Go home, Alex!"

4

The Gleason Ghost

Alex froze in the middle of the aisle. Could he possibly have heard what he thought he heard? *Go home, Alex!* He couldn't have imagined it. But how would the ghost know his name?

Unless … Korina! That had to be it. Korina was hiding behind the curtain, trying to scare him. It would be just like her to try and make him look foolish.

"K-K-Korina?" Alex asked, hoping he was right, wishing the *ghost* was nothing more than his fellow detective. "I know it's you. You can come out now."

No one answered. Seconds later another high-pitched moan pierced the silence. "Boooo! Go home, Alex!"

It sure didn't sound like Korina.

Alex had to get out of there. He twirled around and ran toward the door. He pushed it open and ran through the doorway—right into Tobias.

"Alex?" Tobias asked. "You came early. How nice! You can help us set up."

Behind Tobias, Christopher slid inside the theater, then Korina. She shook out her soggy umbrella. "Hello, Alex," she said. She shook off her raincoat.

Alex stared at them. Korina was standing there, in front of him. Okay. Then who was behind the curtain?

"Alex," Christopher said, "are you all right? You look funny. You didn't have to come so early, you know. You look like you could have used the extra sleep."

"Early? I'm not early," Alex said. "You're late!"

Christopher turned to Korina. "Korina," he said, "didn't you call and tell Alex we changed the rehearsal time to nine?"

Korina shrugged. "I was too busy practicing my song."

"Sorry, Alex," Christopher said, drying his camera case with his sweatshirt sleeve. "But as long as you're here, you can—"

Alex grabbed Christopher's sleeve and pulled him toward the stage. "Hurry! You have to look behind the curtain. I think there's a ghost! It knows my name, and it has Sherlock! Maybe it's eating poor Sherlock for breakfast right now!"

"Alex," Christopher said, letting himself be dragged along, "you're not making any sense."

"Sounds to me as if our youngest detective is jumping to conclusions again," Korina scolded.

Alex rattled off everything that had happened. "So unless this isn't the real Korina," he concluded, pointing to Korina, "*that* Korina is a ghost!"

"Nonsense," Tobias said, unpacking a big bag of props.

"I assure you, I *am* the real Korina," she said. She pulled out her magnifying glass and followed Alex and Christopher to the stage. "But I shall be happy to get to the bottom of your little mystery, Alex."

Just as Alex set foot on the stage, Sherlock flew out from behind the velvet curtains. "*Braawk!*" said Sherlock, zooming in for a smooth landing on Korina's shoulder.

"That's one mystery solved, Alex," Korina said. "Here's your ghost."

Sherlock squawked. "*Booo! Booo!*"

Christopher and Korina broke up laughing. But Alex didn't laugh. He knew Sherlock wasn't the ghost. Someone or something had been behind that curtain. Something eerie had warned him: "*Go home, Alex!*"

"Hallo! Is anybody here?" Ms. Dusic entered through a back door. Rain poured in with her. She slammed the door and shut out the storm. "What a day!" she said, taking off her plastic rain hat and folding it like a fan.

Alex thought Ms. Dusic looked kind of like a female Tobias, but her hair was gray, instead of white. And she didn't smile as much as Tobias did.

"Hello, Ms. Dusic!" Tobias said, coming to help her off with her raincoat. "Aren't you generous to come out in this storm! This show will mean so much for the kids at the center."

Ms. Dusic sighed and looked around the theater. "My, it's worse than I thought." She shivered. "What a dreary place, Tobias. Do you think we can get people to come to the show here?"

"We'll advertise, Ms. Dusic," Christopher said, jumping off the stage. His camera flopped around his neck. "I'll take pictures of rehearsals and post them around the city."

The door flew open and a crowd of kids shoved inside. Alex recognized Danny, April, Tonya, Katy, Cora, and Josh.

"Sorry we're late," April said. "Mom picked everybody up." She threw her raincoat on one of the seats. "Danny was still asleep."

Danny yawned. He still looked half-asleep.

"Outta the way!" Will barged into the theater, making the others scurry to keep from getting run over. Shaking his raincoat so it splattered all over Alex, Will said, "Well, look who's here! The star of the show." He faked a bow, waving his raincoat to douse Alex again. Then in a whisper, he said, "You're going to be sorry, Alex. You're going to wish you'd never won the lead. I promise you that."

"Come on, Will," Alex pleaded. "I *wanted* you to win the lead. Honest!"

But he was talking to the back of Will's head. Will stomped down the aisle to the stage where Ms. Dusic was setting sheet music on the piano. "What a dump!" he said so loud it echoed through the theater.

"Let's see if Ms. Dusic needs our help, Will," Tobias said, catching up with him.

Ms. Dusic glanced up from her music bag. She set out a brown, wooden triangle about the size of a man's foot. "I never go anywhere without my rhythm," she said.

The kids moved toward the stage. Alex trailed along, figuring there might be safety in numbers. The ghost wouldn't come out with the whole cast there. Still, he peered into the corners of the stage and patted the folds in the heavy curtain. Dust flew out, like brown snowflakes. Alex coughed and ran to join the others.

"That's a metronome, isn't it?" Katy asked, pointing to Ms. Dusic's triangular box. "My piano teacher uses one."

"Very good, Katy," said Ms. Dusic. The front of the triangle housed a metal arm in the center. She tapped the arm. It jerked to the left, then to the right. Back and forth. *Click, clunk. Click, clunk.*

Will stopped the metal bar with his finger. "If *I* had the lead role in this stupid musical, we wouldn't need help keeping time," he said. "Besides, I don't see why we have to perform in this dump."

Christopher snapped a picture of the metronome. "Hey," he said, "this place is perfect! You guys will sound great. Your voices will bounce off the rafters!"

"You're right, Christopher," Tobias said, still thumbing through the papers in his bag. "And the important thing is that we raise money to help keep the Youth Center open." He dumped his bag out onstage, then sighed. "I can't find my copy of Christopher's script. I'm sorry, everybody. I'll have to go back to Puzzleworks. I'll be back as fast as I can." Tobias hurried out into the rain.

"I don't know. This theater *is* pretty spooky," Katy said. She and April and Tonya huddled together, as if they were still sharing an umbrella.

"Yes, well," Ms. Dusic said, wiping cobwebs off the piano bench, "the old Gleason wasn't my first choice either. But as far as it being spooky, you shouldn't listen to The Gleason ghost stories."

The theater grew quiet. Then Will asked in his angry voice, "What Gleason ghost stories?"

Ms. Dusic looked surprised. "You mean you haven't heard of The Gleason ghost?"

Korina had been examining a spider she'd found dangling from a high rafter. She lowered her magnifying glass and suddenly looked interested. "Gleason ghost?" she repeated. "Please tell us the story, Ms. Dusic."

Ms. Dusic smiled. "All right then," she said. "Pull me up a folding chair there and I'll tell you what I know."

Christopher dragged over a chair, and Ms. Dusic sat down. One by one, the kids dropped to the floor and sat cross-legged, staring up at their music director. Alex tried to sit as close to Christopher as possible. Tobias had never mentioned the ghost. Even Alex's grandfather had never told him the story of how The Gleason got haunted. And to be honest, Alex wasn't at all sure he wanted to know.

5

The Ghost of Gleason Past

"Now you realize," said Ms. Dusic, "I'm just passing on the tale as it was told to me. It's nothing more than a story … most likely," she said, peering into the overhead rafters. "Still, there are those who say it's all perfectly true.

"There once lived a man—nigh onto 50 years ago—known to be the most talented man in the county. Some would say the most talented man who ever lived. In those days, The Gleason was a beautiful sight to behold. It was the home of a fine opera. People came from miles around to the famous theater."

Ms. Dusic slowly moved her head from side to side, surveying The Gleason. "It was not at all as it is now," she said. She brushed dirt off her long, black skirt. "The man's name was Jeremiah Gleason."

Katy interrupted. "Gleason? Like the theater? Was the theater named after him?"

"No, dear," said Ms. Dusic. "Though I think it may have been named for his great-grandfather, who donated money to the opera."

"So this Jeremy guy got his job because he was related to Old Man Gleason?" Will asked, still sounding angry. "Just like Alex got *his* job because he's part of Christopher's Puzzle Club."

"That's not the way it was," Christopher said. "I didn't even—"

"Boys, boys," said Ms. Dusic. "Shall I go on with the story?"

All the kids shouted, "Yes! Please go on, Ms. Dusic!" All except Alex.

"Jeremiah Gleason seemed to live a charmed life. They say he could play the piano like Mozart and play the trumpet like Gabriel himself. When he sang, you'd believe a choir of angels had joined him. The fame of The Gleason owed much to the fact that Jeremiah Gleason appeared there.

"On top of a brilliant career, Jeremiah had the most beautiful woman as his fiancée, the lovely Miss Roxanne. They became engaged during a run of the successful opera *Marriage of Figaro*. Yes, it seemed that there was none so blessed as Jeremiah Gleason."

"What happened to him?" Korina asked.

Ms. Dusic's mouth turned down, and her eyes took on a sad, teary look. "A talent like Jeremiah's doesn't come along often. He could have gone to New York and had the whole world as his stage. He would have, too, if it had not been for that one fateful night about 50 years ago."

Thunder boomed outside the theater. Tonya gasped, and Cora jumped. "What fateful night?" Will asked.

Alex looked around at the wide-eyed faces staring at Ms. Dusic. She shook her head and continued. "In this particular musical that was being performed ..." She stopped. "Odd," she said. "I hadn't thought of that. It was a musical, not unlike the one we're performing. In fact, it may even have been called *Musical Madness*."

The stage grew still as the kids soaked up the idea that they were putting on a musical like Jeremiah's. Alex knew that must be what had made the ghost so upset.

Ms. Dusic continued. "A new actor moved to the city just for the show—Rathbone, by name. A handsome man, he made the ladies swoon. Now, don't misunderstand me, Jeremiah Gleason was handsome in his own right. But next to Rathbone, not even he could stand.

"They should have known things were about to take a bad turn when the lead role was given, not to the talented Jeremiah, but to Rathbone. The director felt the audience could not help but feel the romance with this new, young star.

"Jeremiah was hurt, embarrassed, and angry. Yet he might still have let this slight pass but for the next misfortune. The female lead, of course, was played by the beautiful Roxanne. In the central scene, she was to be sung to by Rathbone. The scene ended with a tender kiss.

"Rathbone and Roxanne got caught up in the scene's emotion—in particular, its ending. After the final dress rehearsal, Jeremiah discovered his love in the arms of Rathbone, practicing that kiss over and over."

April giggled. "Smooching, right?"

Everybody giggled. Except Alex.

"In that instant, they say Jeremiah Gleason gave in to madness. As a boy, Jeremiah had wandered the secret rooms of the great opera house. Now, he retreated into its darkest corners.

"That night, Jeremiah Gleason terrorized the actors and audience with unspeakable deeds." Ms. Dusic shuddered. "People ran, screaming, from the opera, never to return. Not another performance was given on this stage."

Everybody looked at the stage on which they sat. Alex went cold with fear, afraid to risk a glance at the velvet curtain.

"For the next year," said Ms. Dusic, "no one saw Jeremiah Gleason, but many saw his mischief inside The Gleason. The opera had to close its doors. No one ever heard from Jeremiah again. Those whose minds are of a fanciful nature will tell you the ghost of Jeremiah Gleason lives here still. He haunts the opera house, waiting for his Roxanne."

Nobody spoke. Alex knew that he had the answer to his mystery. That morning, he had met the ghost of Jeremiah Gleason.

6

Harmful Harmony

A stillness hung over The Gleason Theater. Even the thunder had stopped by the time Ms. Dusic finished her ghost story. Suddenly the door flew open. "It's The Gleason ghost!" screamed Katy.

But it was only Tobias. "Katy?" asked Tobias. "Oh, I see. You must have started practice. Go right ahead."

Christopher leaped to action. "Ms. Dusic, please. Tonya, Cora, April, Katy!" he yelled. "Quartet number first!"

Ms. Dusic took her seat at the piano and plinked on the keyboard. "It's flat," she said. "I can't believe this is where they want us to put on our show." She blew dust off the keys.

The quartet members scurried to center stage. Tobias showed them where to stand, then nodded for Christopher and Ms. Dusic to carry on.

"Alex," Christopher said. "We need the music for 'Somewhere over the Monsters.' The music folders are in the back. Good thing I left them here overnight. At least our music should be dry."

With Sherlock on his shoulder, Alex raced down the aisle, grateful not to be called on to sing first. Maybe they wouldn't even get to him. In the last row, Alex spotted a pile of folders. "Which ones?" he shouted back.

"Just Katy's, Cora's, April's, and Tonya's," Christopher said.

Each notebook had a white label with somebody's name on it. Alex saw his and shoved it to the bottom of the pile. Finally, he found all four and ran them back to Christopher.

"Thanks," Christopher said, reaching down to get the notebooks. He passed each one to the appropriate singer, who took it as if it were a Christmas present.

The girls poured over their lyrics. "Cool, Chris," April said. When they'd had a few minutes to read over their parts, Tobias gave the signal to begin.

Ms. Dusic tapped the metal arm on her metronome, sending it back and forth. *Click, clunk.* "Listen for the beat of the music," she said.

She played the piece through. It was "Somewhere over the Rainbow," but Alex knew Christopher had made up better words. Ms. Dusic was playing it fast enough to make a marching band pass out. "I'll at least ask them to get us a good piano," she said. "Honestly!"

She turned to the quartet and smiled. "Don't worry about anyone except yourself as you sing," Ms. Dusic said. "If you sing your part correctly, you will sing well as a group. Harmony is the name of the game. Are we ready?"

They said they were. Ms. Dusic played a long introduction, then nodded for the singers to jump in.

"Music tonight ..." Katy sang.

"There are monsters ..." sang Tonya.

"Deep in the darkness and ..." sang Cora.

"Ahhh-hhhh, I see a ghost ..." April sang.

Each one sang loudly. They may have been okay, if they hadn't been singing together. Words and voices and piano clanged and scraped together in the most horrible sounds Alex had ever heard.

Ms. Dusic stopped. She turned to the singers. "What on earth was that?"

Christopher ran to the quartet. "You guys must be looking at the wrong song. Try it again. This time, stay with the piano."

Ms. Dusic played the introduction, then nodded for the quartet to jump in. They jumped in. But if anything, the noise was even worse this time. It sounded like they were yelling at one another.

"I'm doing it right," Cora said. "I don't know what's wrong with them."

"No way!" Katy said. "You're singing the wrong words. *I've* got it right."

They argued and yelled, each one claiming to have sung the right words.

Tobias had to break up the fight. "I-It will all be fine," he said. "Let's not forget why we're putting on this play. We just need to practice ... a lot."

"Let me see those," Christopher said, taking the folders from the girls. He flipped through the music while the girls glared at one another. "Hey, these are all wrong." Christopher yelled down to Alex, "Alex, did you get the wrong folders? These aren't my lyrics."

Before Alex could answer, Christopher said, "No, these are my folders all right." He studied each sheet of music, his puzzled look deepening.

"What is it, Christopher?" Ms. Dusic asked. "What's wrong?"

Christopher studied each piece of music. "Wait a minute," he said. "Somebody's erased my lyrics and written in different words!"

"Are you sure, Christopher?" Tobias asked.

"Perhaps we should move to the next number while Christopher straightens this out," suggested Ms. Dusic. She glanced at her watch.

"I'm next!" Korina called. She ran to the back of the auditorium and found her own folder and Will's. Then she scrambled up onstage, looking ready to go. "Come on, Will!"

As Will ambled to center stage, Alex slumped in a sticky theater seat and hoped this was a very long duet—too long to get to his song today.

Korina smiled over the empty theater, as if her adoring fans sat waiting. Will scowled, as if he were The Gleason ghost. Ms. Dusic played a few bars of what sounded like "You Are My Sunshine." Then she gave the cue to sing.

Korina opened her notebook and sang in a squeaky voice. "I am so stupid, so very stupid. I am the dumbest girl I know—Hey!" She stopped singing.

Will was laughing so hard, you could hardly hear Korina. The quartet chuckled, trying to hold in giggles.

"That's not funny, Christopher!" Korina said. "I'm not going to sing that, no matter what you say."

Christopher was already onstage. He grabbed the music out of Korina's hands. "I did not write this, Korina," he said. "Somebody's trying to wreck our *Musical Monster Madness,* and I'm going to find out who!"

7

Shadow Man

"They're all ruined!" Christopher said, fingering through the stack of notebooks. "All of them! Look, Alex. Your solo is wrecked!"

Alex wanted to feel sorry for Christopher, but maybe this was his big chance. "Christopher," he said. "I don't need to do a solo. That's okay. Just forget about it."

"No, Alex," Christopher said. "I'll redo every one of these songs, even if it takes me all night."

"Thatta boy!" said Tobias. "Don't forget, everybody. The Youth Center is counting on us."

"Tobias," said Ms. Dusic, "could you drive me home? Perhaps we might discuss a better location for the play?" Ms. Dusic looked around The Gleason. "In the meantime, everybody just be careful!"

Alex watched them leave. Why couldn't Tobias think of some other way to raise money for the Youth Center? Something that didn't involve ghosts or making him look stupid. He was leaving when he saw something move in the back of the theater. A shadow. "Look!" he cried. "A ghost!"

Katy screamed. Tonya started crying.

Alex looked to Korina. He hoped to hear her say, as she always said to him, that he was jumping to conclusions. Instead, she stared wide-eyed at the rear of the theater.

Christopher whipped out his camera. He aimed and snapped. The flash of his lightbulb revealed a dark figure in the corner of The Gleason. Christopher flashed again and again. The figure appeared, then disappeared, like magic.

"Who's there?" Korina called, her voice shaking.

"It's Jeremiah Gleason," Alex whispered.

"Come on out!" said Will, stepping in front of Alex. "*I'm* not afraid of an old ghost!"

The figure stepped out of the shadow. Alex saw a wrinkled trench coat, topped by a broad brimmed hat that was pulled low over the man's forehead. You could barely see his face. He was tall, lean, and as old as Alex's dad.

"What are you doing back there?" Christopher asked.

The quartet girls were huddled together between the rows of theater seats. April stood up and pointed at the man. "I know you!" she said. "My dad works for you. You're Mr. Riley."

Mr. Riley nodded.

Riley. Alex tried to remember where he'd heard that name before. *Riley. Riley.* It was no use. He was so scared, he could hardly remember his own name.

"What were you doing back there?" Will asked, his fists still clenched.

Christopher stepped up and introduced himself. "This is the cast of *Musical Monster Madness.* You'll have to excuse us. Too many ghost stories. I guess we're kind of nervous about putting on our first real play."

"I heard you were putting this show on in The Gleason," Mr. Riley said. "I couldn't believe it. Had to see it with my own eyes. Do you really think anyone will come to see your play in this old building? The Gleason should be condemned. Knocked down, if you ask me."

Christopher started to explain. "There aren't too many buildings we could get for free. And besides, I think people will come—"

But Mr. Riley interrupted, his face twisted into a sinister smirk that gave Alex the chills. "We'll just see about that," he said. Then he slipped out the back door.

"He's spooky," said Katy, pulling her coat tight around her. "I'm getting out of here."

The rest of the kids followed her out. Korina and Alex helped Christopher gather the folders. "We'll take them to Puzzle Club headquarters so I can redo them," Christopher said.

"We can dust for fingerprints too," Korina said. "Maybe we can come up with who changed the words."

Alex didn't say anything. He knew he didn't need to run any experiments to find out who had messed up Christopher's music. It was Jeremiah Gleason. And that ghost wasn't going to rest until he'd put an end to *Musical Monster Madness.*

Next morning Alex biked to headquarters. He had promised to meet Christopher and Korina there before play practice. As he parked his bike, he heard Ms. Dusic's voice inside Puzzleworks.

"The rumors are all over town, Tobias," she was saying as Alex walked inside. "But if you're determined to stick with The Gleason, I'm sure we'll survive somehow. Right, Alex?" Ms. Dusic scurried out the door.

"Survive?" Alex repeated. He didn't like the sound of the word.

"*Brawk! Survive!*" Sherlock repeated from his perch on Tobias' cash register.

"Alex," Tobias said, "Ms. Dusic believes *Musical Monster Madness* is in trouble. Who would have spoiled Christopher's music? The Puzzle Club has to solve this mystery, Alex. If this show doesn't come off, we can say good-bye to the Youth Center."

Tobias looked so sad. In Alex's fear about performing, he'd forgotten why Christopher and Tobias had started this show. Alex knew plenty of kids who went to the center every day after school and on weekends. Tobias said for some of them it was the only place they had to go. The people who ran the center did more with the kids than just crafts and games. Alex knew they helped with homework and told the kids about people like Noah, King David, Paul, and especially, Jesus.

Tobias ran his fingers through his white hair. "You know what this means to boys like Will, Alex. You have to help get to the bottom of all this."

"Okay, Tobias," Alex said. He'd still do all he could to get out of performing, but he'd help make sure everybody else did perform. For the sake of Tobias and the Youth Center, the show had to go on … as long as it went on without him.

"You better get up to headquarters, Alex," Tobias said. He pulled the gold cord behind his counter, and the secret shelf slid aside. Alex ran upstairs and pushed open the door to Puzzle Club headquarters. The minute he heard the siren, Alex realized he'd forgotten to punch in the secret code.

Whoop … whoop … whoop went the alarm.

"*Squawk … squawk … squawk!*" said Sherlock, zooming in behind Alex.

"Alex!" Korina scolded.

Alex quickly punched in the alarm code and the sirens stopped. "Got it," he said.

"Nice going, Alex," Korina said. She sat at her examination table, sheets of music laid out in front of her. Korina held a magnifying glass in each hand. The lenses were trained on different sheets. Her head bobbed from one magnifying glass to the other.

Christopher was hanging up his photographs, clothespinning them to a line that stretched the width of the attic. "Hey, Alex," he said, "I haven't found anything in the photos yet."

"I just wish I had a copy of everyone's fingerprints," Korina said. She shook fingerprint powder over a folder. "Of course, it wouldn't help much now, the way we all handled the music. Still, I have a sneaking suspicion I might discover Will's fingerprints at the bottom of this."

"Will?" Alex asked. "Why Will?"

"In case you failed to notice, Mr. Detective," Korina said, as if talking to a little kid, "Will is not exactly happy with *Musical Monster Madness*. He wanted *your* part. I think he'd do anything to scare the rest of us off. Then he could do the whole show himself."

"Will wrecked Christopher's music?" Alex asked.

"Now, Korina," Christopher said.

"I am not jumping to conclusions," said Korina. "But for the sake of *Musical Monster Madness,* I believe we should keep an eye on Will."

8

Shadow That Shadow

Leaving Sherlock at headquarters, Christopher, Korina, and Alex took a shortcut through downtown to The Gleason. They had just pulled up to the theater when out the door flew Tonya, April, and Katy, screaming at the top of their lungs.

"It's the ghost!" yelled Katy.

"It's that Jerry Gleason guy!" April screamed.

"Whoa," Christopher said. "Wait! What's going on?"

The girls glanced at one another. Then Tonya let words spill out fast. "We were sitting in The Gleason, minding our own business, waiting for you, when all of a sudden, we heard ..." She broke down and covered her face with her hands.

"We heard Jeremiah Gleason," Katy said, "playing his trumpet."

"Playing his trumpet?" Korina asked.

The three girls nodded their heads seven or eight times.

Alex didn't want to go inside.

"Hey! What's happening?" It was Will, coming around the corner of The Gleason.

Will. *Will* plays the trumpet, Alex remembered.

"Where did you come from, Will?" Korina asked.

Will squinted at her. "Home. Where'd you think I came from? Mars, like you?"

"It's The Gleason ghost!" Katy warned. "Don't go in there, Will."

"Ghost, toast," Will said. Opening the door and stepping inside, he said, "*I'm* not afraid."

Somehow Christopher talked everyone into going back inside the theater. "If we hear anything scary," Christopher said, "I'll personally walk all of you girls home."

Ms. Dusic and Tobias arrived, and practice got underway. Ms. Dusic set out her metronome and began with the quartet. This time, their voices sounded shaky, but the words fit together at least. Alex figured Christopher must have stayed up all night redoing the music.

Korina asked to go next. She and Will sang their whole song without looking at the music. Alex thought maybe Korina *should* look at the music. She knew the words, but her notes did not quite match Will's or the piano's. Will's strong voice almost drowned out Korina though, and it didn't sound half bad.

Danny and Josh goofed off during their number. Finally, it was Alex's turn. Ms. Dusic called his name. Alex stayed put. Korina yelled for him. Then Christopher came down and whispered, "Do it for Tobias, Alex."

Alex looked at Tobias onstage and got to his feet. He heard the clicking of Ms. Dusic's metronome, then the piano, as he moved toward the microphone. Alex opened his mouth and hoped something would come out. "I'm looking for a monster," he sang. He knew it was too soft. "Is there a monster ..."

Before he could finish, as if in answer, a howling burst from the walls of The Gleason. A violin played a haunting melody that froze the cast of *Musical Monster Madness*. The whine of violin strings filled the air.

"Aaah!" screamed Cora. "The ghost of The Gleason!" Then she, Tonya, April, and Katy raced out of the theater with Danny and Josh close behind.

Alex didn't wait for Korina or Christopher. He ran for the exit and pushed open the door. Sunlight blinded him. Then, *thud!* Alex smashed into somebody—somebody a lot bigger than he was. Slowly Alex raised his eyes until he could see who it was. He recognized the man they'd met the day before in the back of The Gleason. "Mr. Riley?"

"Alex! Come back!" Christopher bolted out of the theater and bumped into the back of Alex. He stopped and stared at Mr. Riley.

Korina burst out, bumped into Christopher, who bumped Alex, who bumped Mr. Riley. "Mr. Riley," she said, "what are you doing here?"

"Me?" he asked. "I'm, er, I just stopped to see if you people got a better building. That's all."

"We didn't," Alex said. "And this one's haunted!"

"Alex," Korina said. "Don't jump to conclusions."

"That's too bad," Mr. Riley said. He sounded like he meant it. "You're making a big mistake trying to revive The Gleason." His glare felt like ice. For a minute, Alex considered running back to the ghost. Then Mr. Riley turned and walked stiffly away.

"Wh-what do you think he meant by that?" Alex asked, staring after the man.

"I don't know, Alex," Christopher said. "But I'd like to find out. Let's follow him."

Christopher led, and Korina followed. There wasn't anything left for Alex to do but follow Korina. They ducked behind buildings and bushes. Mr. Riley kept looking over his shoulder, so they couldn't get too close.

After they'd trailed him for about a block, Christopher shoved Korina and Alex back into an alley. "Stay back," he whispered. "Mr. Riley was turning around." They held their breaths and didn't make a sound. Finally, Christopher peeked around the corner at the end of the alley. "He didn't come back this way," said Christopher. "But now I think we've lost him."

Alex and Korina stepped out of the alley and looked for Mr. Riley too. They were just about to give up and go back to Puzzle Club headquarters when something across the street caught Alex's eye. The sign. He'd passed that sign before! That's where he'd heard the name *Riley!* "Christopher! Korina!" he shouted, running across the street.

Christopher and Korina came running after him. Alex raced to the deserted lot only a block from The Gleason. A crumbly, broken-down brick building stood alone in a pile of rubble. In front of the building a sign read: *New Greater City Shopping Mall Coming Soon! Riley Developers.*

"See!" Alex said. He took out his pencil and copied the words into his detective's notepad. "I knew I'd seen that name ..."

Somebody pushed Alex from behind. He fell forward.

"Duck!" Christopher fell on top of Alex. Korina was between them.

Alex squirmed to get off the bottom of the pile. He rolled over ... just in time to see why Christopher had pushed him out of the way. A giant wrecking ball, as big as the moon, swung over them and crashed into the old building behind them.

With a boom like thunder, the walls came tumbling down. Bricks and dust flew everywhere. Alex covered his eyes.

"Hey! Are you kids okay?" A burly man in a yellow hard hat ran up to them. Then two more workers came from across the street. "What were you kids doing here? You could have been hurt!"

Alex coughed. Korina and Christopher looked okay. Alex closed his eyes and said a quick prayer of thanks. When he opened his eyes, he saw the wrecking crane in the distance. A long chain led to the hill of scattered bricks where the huge ball lay.

Alex squinted to see who was driving the crane. It wasn't anybody he'd seen before. But the man talking to the driver sure looked familiar. "Hey," Alex said, letting himself be pulled up by the man in the hard hat. "That man over there, next to the wrecking crane. Who is that?"

"Him? That's our boss," said the worker. "Mr. Riley."

9

Will He, or Won't He?

Alex was still shaking as they climbed the secret staircase to Puzzle Club headquarters. Tobias had fussed over them for an hour until they had convinced him they weren't hurt.

"It looks to me like we have a new number 1 suspect," Christopher said, unloading his camera. "We don't want to jump to conclusions, but Mr. Riley has a lot to gain if our show flops. The Gleason stands in the way of his big shopping mall. So does the Youth Center. He probably wants to knock the buildings down like he's wrecked everything else downtown."

"Yeah," Alex said. "And like he tried to wreck us." He shivered again, just thinking about it.

"We don't know that he meant to hurt us, Alex," Christopher said. "We shouldn't have run over where they were tearing things down. And we should have paid more attention to what was going on around us."

Korina was searching through her box of experiments. "I haven't given up my suspicions about Will," she said. "We still have to explain the mystery of The Gleason ghost. Mr. Riley can't play the trumpet, for one thing. Will can. I'd like to follow Will and see what he's up to. Tobias said he got Will to promise he would go to the Youth Center today. Maybe we can catch up with him there."

"I have to work on the script," Christopher said. "Alex, can you take this assignment with Korina?"

Alex shrugged. He didn't have anything better to do. And he'd rather tail Will than Jeremiah Gleason any day.

Christopher sat in the rocking chair by the attic window with the music on his lap. Pulling out a pencil, he went to work as Sherlock took a free ride on the back of the rocker. Alex crossed the room to his rack of disguises. He considered the businessman, the construction worker, and the baker before deciding on his teacher costume.

"Come on, Alex," Korina said. "What are you doing over there?"

"We both need disguises, Korina." He pulled on the jacket. It was kind of hot, but better than the animal costumes.

"I don't want a disguise," said Korina.

"I think Alex is right," Christopher said. "You should wear a disguise, Korina. What if Will sees you?"

Alex loved it when Christopher agreed with him instead of Korina. "Here," he told her, holding up a shirt he'd just bought at a church rummage sale. "You can dress up as a farmer."

Korina slipped into the flannel shirt and overalls. Alex put a beard and bushy eyebrows on her and completed the disguise with a big, straw hat. "Are you sure I look like a farmer?" she asked.

Christopher cleared his throat. He was probably thinking what Alex was thinking. Korina looked more like a scarecrow than a farmer. "Uh … Will won't recognize you, Korina. That's for sure," Christopher said.

Korina stretched out her arms to pull her sleeves up. Sherlock flew and landed on one outstretched arm. Alex held his breath to keep from laughing. Now she *really* looked like a scarecrow.

Korina shooed Sherlock away, then beat Alex to the secret chute. She pressed the center of the big private eye symbol and climbed onto the slide. "Farmers first!" she shouted.

In 10 minutes Alex and Korina were at the Youth Center. They locked their bikes and entered through the side door. They walked past four teenage boys who were laughing and slapping a shorter kid on the back. Alex almost forgot he and Korina were in disguise, until he saw the way the boys stared at them. Alex smiled nervously and tried to look like a teacher. As soon as Alex and Korina passed the group of boys, laughter exploded behind them.

Once inside, Korina and Alex followed the sounds of squeaking tennis shoes and bouncing basketballs to the gym. Two half-court games were in progress. Each had a referee who blew the whistle about every two seconds. Kids yelled and pushed one another, just like out on the street, Alex thought. But at least here they had referees. And most fights ended with quiet talks—and if Tobias were in on it, prayer. Alex knew several kids who had started going to church because of Tobias' actions on the basketball courts.

Alex and Korina searched the entire center. They saw April and Katy and Josh—but no Will. "Guess Will didn't keep his promise to Tobias," Korina said. "We'll have to go to his apartment. He lives over in Moriarty Green." She rolled up her long pant legs and adjusted her coat.

Alex followed Korina down Lexington to Bascomb Road. A shiver came over Alex as they passed Bascomb Mansion. Alex used to think that mansion was the scariest place in the city, but that was before he'd gone inside The Gleason.

Korina wound through back alleys and across thoroughfares. Alex wasn't sure where they were until they bounced across the railroad tracks. Then it was too late. This was the part of the city his mother called "rough." As many people lived in these few blocks as in miles around Alex's neighborhood.

"That's Moriarty Green," Korina said, jumping off her moving bike.

Shirtless boys played basketball on a gravel court. The shuffling spit of shoes on gravel joined with yelling and barking dogs. It smelled like a dumpster. Three little kids dug in the dirt with broken plastic beach toys. A couple of girls bigger than Korina fought over a jump rope. Their words clashed with the sharper words of a mother screaming at her son to come inside.

"I don't see Will," Alex said. "Let's go back."

"Alex," Korina scolded. "Don't tell me you're scared of Moriarty Green."

"Of course not," Alex said. "I just don't know which apartment is Will's."

"Stay with the bikes," Korina said. "I'll find Will's apartment."

Korina went from kid to kid, asking questions. Finally, a boy pointed to one of the windows. Korina waved for Alex to join her. Alex pushed both bikes, wishing she'd come get hers. They locked the bikes to a metal bar under the stairwell.

Korina led the way, and Alex followed. He grabbed the metal railing, and goo stuck to his fingers. Alex felt gum sticking to the soles of his shoes.

Suddenly, Korina elbowed Alex in the chest. "Hide!" she said. Then she jumped over the railing and pulled Alex with her.

Alex landed on one knee. It stung. "Korina!" he said.

Korina slapped her hand over his mouth. "Shh-h-h."

Alex's chest hurt. His knee throbbed. He wanted to go home.

Like metal drums, *bong, bong, bong,* came the thump of shoes on the metal stairs. Somebody plunked down, skipping the last three steps and landing on the sidewalk. All Alex saw were sneakers running off.

"That's him!" Korina said. "That's Will. After him!" Korina unlocked her bike and jumped on in one smooth motion.

Alex fumbled with his lock, then jumped on his bike and followed her. "Wait up!" he hollered. He was pedaling as fast as he could. Still, Korina's figure grew smaller and smaller ahead of him.

Instead of slowing down, Korina waved her arm for Alex to catch up. To Alex, all the streets looked the same. Even the apartment houses, big cement blocks, looked alike. He wondered if people ever got mixed up and went in the wrong house. He didn't want to get lost. Alex stood on his pedals to help pick up speed.

It wasn't until he rounded a corner that he figured out where they were going. Downtown. They weren't that far from The Gleason. Maybe that's where Will was headed. If they could catch Will red-handed, rigging up some prank in the theater, then they'd have their proof. They could solve this case before the curtain went up on *Musical Monster Madness*.

Alex looked up from his bike. Korina had disappeared. He glanced around, but she was gone. What if Will had grabbed her? Or Jeremiah Gleason? Or ...

"Pssst." Korina hissed at Alex from behind a parked truck. She was crouched low, looking around the loading dock. "Here," she whispered.

Alex hopped off his bike and joined her. "What's—"

"Get down," she said, pointing across the street.

Alex looked, and there was Will, checking to the left, checking to the right, then dashing inside a metal trailer, a makeshift office.

They waited until Will disappeared inside. Then they crossed the street to check it out. "Alex!" Korina called. "Take a look at this."

Alex ran over to Korina. She was reading the name on the door of the trailer. Big black letters read: *J.G. Riley, Developers.*

10

There's No Business Like Show Business

Back at headquarters, Korina and Alex related their adventures to Christopher. Korina finished, out of breath. "So it is rather obvious that Will and Mr. Riley are in this together. Will wants revenge. And Mr. Riley wants The Gleason and the Youth Center knocked down so he can build his shopping mall."

"I know Will wanted a bigger part in the show," Christopher said. "But I can't believe he'd stoop to this."

The Puzzle Club agreed to keep a close watch on Will during practices the rest of the week. But it didn't help. New disasters met *Musical Monster Madness* every day at rehearsals. First, the doors of The Gleason were locked from the inside. The cast missed a whole day of practice. That wasn't so bad, Alex thought. But the next day, they all got locked *inside* The Gleason. If Korina hadn't managed to climb out a bathroom window, Alex didn't know what might have become of them.

The only good thing about the week was that Tobias put Alex in charge of costumes. If he did say so himself—and he did—Alex did a super job getting everybody an outfit for the show. Scary monsters, funny costumes—the cast went nuts over them.

Finally, Friday came, the day before the show. In the morning Tobias drove Alex and the costumes to The Gleason for the dress rehearsal that night. "Pray for the Youth Center, Alex," Tobias said as they parked in front of The Gleason. "We want that audience to give, give, give to the center. And pray for the show to glorify God."

As Alex and Tobias hung up the monster costumes in the deserted theater, Alex couldn't help peering over his shoulder. He half expected The Gleason ghost to leap out at them. Sherlock flew back and forth across the room, as if looking for the ghost.

Tobias stopped what he was doing, then broke out into his Tobias grin. "Hallelujah!" he shouted. All over the empty Gleason, Tobias' shout echoed: *Hallelujah! Hallelujah! Hallelujah!*

Alex laughed. *Even Jeremiah Gleason wouldn't be a match for Tobias,* he thought.

Friday night Alex stood onstage with the cast of *Musical Monster Madness.* Christopher gathered everyone for a pep talk. "This is dress rehearsal, everybody," he said. "I want you to act as if it's the real thing. Tomorrow night it will be!"

"Hey!" Will called from the rack of costumes. "What's the matter with this monster suit?"

"What are you talking about?" Alex asked, going over to Will.

"I can't get into it." Will kept raising his foot to his Frankenstein costume, then stepping down again. "You forgot to leave an opening, Alex."

"I did not," Alex said. He grabbed the costume out of Will's hands. The back had been sewn shut.

"What happened to my dress?" screamed Katy. She held up the hanger with what used to be her princess costume. Now it looked like a "before" picture of Cinderella's dress. Ugly, gray patches had been sewn to the dress.

"My zipper won't unzip!" said Tonya.

"Look at my costume!" cried April. "Somebody sewed the neck and armholes shut."

Alex ran from costume to costume. Every single one had something wrong with it. "Who did this?" Alex asked and glared at Will.

Ms. Dusic ran up. "Oh dear! Now what will we do? We can't have a show without costumes. We'll have to cancel!"

Tobias stood in the middle of the confusion. Sherlock flapped his wings and flew circles overhead. "B-But we can't cancel!" Tobias said. "The children ... the center ... they're counting on us!"

"Look," Christopher said. "It will be okay. We'll go ahead with the rehearsal. We'll just pretend we have our costumes on. Alex can fix the costumes. Nothing's really ruined. We'll just undo stuff. Come on! On with the show!"

The cast grumbled, but one by one, they took their places, and the rehearsal began. Alex had to admit the first couple of numbers sounded pretty good. Korina must have been practicing. Still, Alex had a weird feeling in the pit of his stomach. He just knew his number wouldn't go so well.

Josh and Danny finished their song and dance. Now it was Alex's turn. He tiptoed to the microphone and felt, rather than saw, Sherlock land on his shoulder. He tried to pray. But as he looked over the empty seats of The Gleason, Alex imagined every seat filled. And every face staring up at him ... laughing at him.

Ms. Dusic played the introduction. Alex was so nervous, he lost his place and couldn't remember when to come in.

"Alex?" asked Ms. Dusic. "Here, let me help you." She played the intro again. Then she stopped. "You'll know it's time to come in when I play this note, Alex. It's the lowest note you'll hear all night. I'll show you on your music." Ms. Dusic plunked the low key on the piano and stepped toward Alex and the microphone.

"Look out!" yelled Christopher.

Alex turned just in time to see a huge sandbag drop from the ceiling and crash onto the piano, inches from Ms. Dusic's head!

11

Musical Madness

The cast of *Musical Monster Madness* gathered around the piano, staring as if hypnotized by the brown sandbag on the keyboard. Sherlock hid his face in Alex's collar.

Finally, Will said, "If you hadn't gotten up and moved, you could have been killed, Ms. Dusic!"

"Are you all right?" Tobias asked, rushing to Ms. Dusic's side. "I'm so thankful you weren't hurt!"

"I knew having the show at The Gleason was a mistake," she said. "I tried to tell you we needed a better, newer building. But you wouldn't listen. And now this!"

The Puzzle Club cleared the stage and sent everyone home. Tobias wanted to drive Ms. Dusic to the hospital, but she insisted on being driven straight home. Then Christopher, Korina, and Alex examined the sandbag. It was the one rigged to pull the stage curtain. Christopher clicked photos from every angle. Korina examined the sandbag with her magnifying glass.

Alex nosed around backstage with his notepad. Above the stage a wooden walkway ran the width of The Gleason about 10 feet under the ceiling. Christopher started up the stairs that led to the walkway. Alex was making a list of suspects when he heard Christopher call from the platform above him.

"I found something!" Christopher shouted.

Flashbulbs from Christopher's camera lit the ceiling like stars. Then Christopher came running down the stairs. "I found this behind a speaker up there." He held out a cassette tape. "It's getting late," he said, looking at his watch. "Tomorrow morning we'll meet at Puzzleworks and see if we can find any clues on this tape."

Saturday morning, with 10 hours to curtain time for *Musical Monster Madness,* The

Puzzle Club had a million things to do. They dumped the costumes in Tobias' puzzle corner and sat down to listen to the tape Christopher had found at The Gleason. But after running for almost five minutes, no sound had come from the tape player.

"It's nothing but a blank tape," Alex said, disappointed.

"I really thought I'd found something," Christopher said.

The girls' quartet showed up at Puzzleworks to give Alex a hand with the costumes. Christopher and Korina excused themselves and ran up to headquarters. The girls and Alex went to work un-sewing zippers and armholes. Tonya said her mother almost made her quit the play. Katy wanted a coat of armor for her costume. Sherlock flew from girl to girl, soaking up the extra attention.

After about a half hour, Alex heard a *click, clunk ... click, clunk.* He tried to ignore the sound, but it started to get to him. Finally he said, "Will whoever's making that clicking sound please stop."

"I was just thinking the same thing," Katy said, looking up from the princess costume she was working on.

"It's not me," April said.

Tonya and Cora shrugged. Sherlock flapped his wings. The clicking continued.

Alex listened. The tape player! He picked up the recorder and held it to his ear. The clicking was coming from the recorder. Suddenly, a loud screech burst from the speaker. Alex dropped the recorder and covered his ears. Sherlock screeched and flew out the window.

"That's the ghost!" screamed April. "That's what we heard at The Gleason!"

Tobias appeared from the stockroom. Korina and Christopher ran down from headquarters. "What's that racket?" Korina asked.

Christopher picked up the tape player. "Here's our ghost." As soon as he said it, the violin stopped. All that could be heard was the *click, clunk.* Then even that stopped. Alex started to shut off the tape player, but Christopher stopped him. "We'll take this to headquarters and let it play out," Christopher said. "Maybe more clues will come on."

Alex and the girls finished the costumes. The quartet promised to guard the outfits with their lives and bring them to The Gleason by six that night. Alex thanked them and dashed up to Puzzle Club headquarters.

"Alex," Korina said. "We left the tape running and heard a trumpet playing."

Christopher was studying the photos he'd enlarged and strung above the exam table. "The way we figure it, all the fake ghost had to do was start the tape and leave. Later, when some of the kids got to The Gleason, the violin or trumpet played over the speakers and scared everybody."

"But why?" Alex asked. Alex peered over Christopher's shoulder at the photos. One showed Ms. Dusic playing the piano. Another showed the microphone on The Gleason stage.

"Do you see something strange in these pictures?" Christopher asked. "Look through this." He handed Korina's magnifying glass to Alex.

Alex had to squint for a long time. Then he saw it. A thin line that could have been a crack in the photo. It ran from the piano straight up and out of the picture. He saw another thin line in a picture of the fallen sandbag. That one stretched from the sack across the floor. "What is it?" Alex asked.

"That's what we have to find out," Christopher said. "Go home and get ready. Then meet me at The Gleason at five o'clock."

At five, Alex still sat on the stairs at Puzzleworks. Tobias turned off the lights, leaving Alex in darkness.

"Alex?" Tobias asked, strolling past the secret stairwell. "I thought you were meeting Christopher at The Gleason."

"I can't go, Tobias," Alex said.

Tobias sat on the step below Alex. "Tell me all about it, Alex. Is it the ghost you're afraid of?"

"Yes ... no." Alex hadn't thought it out himself. "I don't think it's the ghost I'm scared of, Tobias. I think it's me. I can't sing. Everybody will make fun of me. They'll think I'm stupid."

"Alex," Tobias said through the darkness of the room. "Remember why we're putting on this play. It's for the Youth Center. It's for God. You don't have to be a star. All you have to do is make a joyful noise."

"Make a what, Tobias?" Alex asked.

" 'Make a joyful noise to the rock of our salvation,' " Tobias said. "It's from the Psalms." Tobias' eyes seemed to drill right through Alex ... into his heart. "Alex, you can make a joyful noise, can't you? That's what counts. And make it to the Lord, no matter who is in that audience."

Alex couldn't argue with Tobias. This play could make a big difference to a lot of kids who counted on the Youth Center. And Alex *could* make a noise. "That's all, Tobias?" Alex felt relief rush through him like water. "A joyful noise?" Tobias nodded. Then Alex tried it. He yelled at the top of his lungs. It was a happy yell, a joyous yell.

Tobias joined in with a loud noise of his own. They yelled until they couldn't anymore because they were laughing so hard. Alex had not laughed for a week, not since Korina had called him chicken. It felt good.

Tobias gave Alex a ride to the theater, which might have started up a whole new set of fears, since Tobias was the worst driver Alex had ever known. When they got to The Gleason, Tobias checked out the sound system while Alex ran to find Christopher and Korina. The stage looked empty. But Alex could make out the sleeping Sherlock nestled in a feathered hat on a costume rack.

"Alex, up here!"

Alex looked straight above the stage. On the little platform, Christopher and Korina were bending over something he couldn't see. Alex took the stairs to the walkway, trying not to look down at the stage. He found Korina and Christopher bending over a bucket of flour. It was set on the edge of the platform. Alex peered straight down to where the microphone stood ready for the first number.

"We found a wire on the piano and traced it up here," Korina said. "That's the line we saw in Christopher's photos. When the right note is played down below, the wire pulls. Then the bucket of flour dumps onto the singers."

"Did The Gleason ghost set this trap?" Alex asked.

"This was no ghost," Christopher said. "I think I know who did it, but I don't know why."

"What are we going to do?" Korina asked.

"We're going to set a ghost trap," Christopher said. "Better yet, make that an untrap."

12

A Reason for The Gleason

The show did go on. One minute before curtain, while Alex and the cast scurried around backstage, the velvet curtain began to wave. Tonya screamed, and Alex was sure he was about to see Jeremiah Gleason.

Instead, Tobias squeezed between the curtains, his face as bright as a lightbulb. "Christopher, Alex, Korina, everybody!" he shouted. "It's a full house! Places everyone!"

Alex would have said something, but his throat felt tight with nerves, and he didn't know if he could talk. Tobias gave him a secret wink. "Remember," Tobias whispered. "A joyful noise."

The curtain opened and the quartet sang their number in full costume. Alex didn't dare peek out at the audience. When the song ended, the applause broke out like thunder. Korina and Will got even more applause! The boys did their song and dance routine. Then it was time for Alex.

"A joyful noise. A joyful noise," Alex mumbled as he took center stage. At first he couldn't see into the theater because of the bright footlights. But as he waited behind the microphone, his eyes got used to the light. Gradually an ocean of faces came into view. Alex thought he'd never seen so many people in his whole life. And they were all looking at him.

For a second, Alex froze. He heard someone in the audience clear her throat. Sheriff Grimaldi coughed. Several chairs squeaked as people squirmed in their seats. Alex couldn't figure out what to do with his hands.

The first note Ms. Dusic played on the piano startled Alex so much, he dropped his music. As he picked it up, he heard the ticking of the metronome as Ms. Dusic pounded out the introduction. He waited for that lowest of all notes. At last it came.

Alex took a breath and sang, "I—"

But the piano didn't play his song. Ms. Dusic had stopped playing. Alex looked over at her. She seemed confused. She smiled, but the smile did funny things on her face. Ms. Dusic played the low note again.

Alex began his song again. But once more, Ms. Dusic stopped playing. "Ms. Dusic?" Alex whispered.

Ms. Dusic pounded the low note. Again and again she played the same note. She pushed back the piano bench with a *screech*. Then she stared up—straight up to where, an hour before, The Puzzle Club had laid its ghost trap!

"Curtain!" Christopher yelled from backstage. Before the curtain closed, he announced to the murmuring audience, "Ladies and gentlemen! Please enjoy this brief intermission." Then the curtain flapped shut.

Backstage, The Puzzle Club gathered around Ms. Dusic. Will ran over and asked, "What's going on?"

"You'll have to ask Ms. Dusic that, Will," Christopher said. "We caught her in a ghost trap."

Ms. Dusic looked as if somebody had just knocked all the air out of her. She slumped back down onto the piano bench and covered her face with her hands.

"You mean Will wasn't the ghost after all?" Korina asked.

"I was pretty sure it was Ms. Dusic as soon as I realized that clicking sound on the tape had to be her metronome," Christopher explained. "But I needed to unset the booby trap she set for tonight, just to be sure."

"You suspected *me*?" Will asked. "Thanks a lot, Korina! What made you think *I* was causing everything?"

"You were mad about not getting the part," Korina said. "You play the trumpet. And we saw you go into Riley Developers. I'm sorry, Will. I thought Mr. Riley had talked you into helping him make sure The Gleason was closed for good so he could put up his shopping mall."

Alex knew it wasn't easy for Korina to apologize.

Will seemed to soften. "Aw, that's okay. Riley did try to get me to wreck the show. That's why he asked me to come to his office. But when he found out I had such a little part, the deal was off. I told him he'd be wasting his time talking to Alex or anybody in The Puzzle Club."

"Did you say Mr. Riley?" Tobias asked. Alex felt a little better about not having come up with the solution himself. Even Korina and Tobias seemed as surprised as he was. Tobias turned to Ms. Dusic. "Are they talking about your brother, Tom Riley?"

"Her brother?" Christopher and Korina said together.

Ms. Dusic nodded without looking up.

Tobias explained. "Ms. Dusic's name used to be Riley—before she got married and moved to New York. But I don't understand. Surely she had nothing to do with this."

Ms. Dusic's shoulders shook as she cried quietly. Alex still couldn't believe she'd been the ghost all along, but it fit. Will wasn't the only one who played the trumpet. And she played the violin. The sandbag had missed her because she'd known exactly when to move away from the piano. "Ms. Dusic, won't you please tell us why you tried to stop the show?" Alex asked.

Ms. Dusic finally looked up at them. "I'm so ashamed. We didn't mean to hurt anyone. The wrecking ball was just an accident—you have to believe me. Tom did want to get rid of this theater so he could build his shopping mall. He promised he would build a modern opera house and let me run it. All I had to do was make sure your show didn't succeed.

"I used to direct symphonies in the finest halls of New York," she said, a faraway look in her eyes. "That's all I wanted—to give New Bristol a decent theater." She looked from one cast member to another. In a whisper, she said, "I see now how wrong I was. Can you ever forgive me?"

"Of course we can" Tobias said.

Christopher was the first to give Ms. Dusic a hug. Then Korina followed suit and all the cast members—even Will.

"Ms. Dusic," Alex said, "you don't have to worry about the audience or the theater. When you're doing what God wants, like raising this money to keep the Youth Center open, all you have to do is make a joyful noise. Tobias taught me that. Make a joyful noise to the Lord."

"Alex is right," Korina said. "Some of us have been so wrapped up in other things—looking good on stage, solving this mystery—we forgot why Tobias started this play.

The Youth Center is more important than anything else."

Tobias put one arm around Alex and one arm around Korina. "How about it, Ms. Dusic?" he asked. "Do you want to help?"

"Oh yes!" she said.

"Well, let's get out there and make a joyful noise!" Christopher shouted. "Alex, you're on! Curtain, everybody!"

It seemed to Alex that Ms. Dusic played the piano more beautifully than he'd ever heard her play. Alex sang his whole solo with Sherlock sitting on his shoulder. Sherlock chimed in several times with his musical squawking, to the delight of the audience. Alex knew he still wasn't a great singer, but somehow that didn't matter. As he finished the last note, he found himself smiling, and the audience smiled back.

At the end of the show, thunderous applause made the cast come back for more bows. The night ended with a standing ovation. At last Christopher took the microphone and invited Tobias to say a few words.

Tobias joined the cast onstage. "On behalf of the cast of *Musical Monster Madness,* I want to thank all of you for coming. Tonight we've raised enough money to keep our Youth Center open for a long time to come. And a special thanks goes to Mr. Riley, of Riley Developers, for his generous donation."

Alex tugged Christopher's sleeve. "Mr. Riley gave money to the center?"

Christopher whispered back, "I believe his big sister, Ms. Dusic, had a heart-to-heart talk with her little brother."

As the crowd broke out into applause one last time, Will leaned over and elbowed Alex. "You know," Will said, "it's kind of a good thing about that center staying open. I think I might like hanging out there with you guys."

Alex took a last look around The Gleason. Somehow all the scariness had gone out of it. As he stood there, Alex may not have been singing on the outside, but inside, he was making a joyful noise to the Lord.